HELLO NEIGHBOR

CUBA

by Jeri Cipriano

LOOK! BOOKS™

Red Chair Press   Egremont, Massachusetts

Look! Books are produced and published by Red Chair Press:
Red Chair Press LLC   PO Box 333   South Egremont, MA 01258-0333
www.redchairpress.com

Publisher's Cataloging-In-Publication Data

Names: Cipriano, Jeri S.

Title: Cuba / by Jeri Cipriano.

Description: Egremont, Massachusetts : Red Chair Press, [2019] | Series: Look! books : Hello neighbor | Interest age level: 004-008. | Includes index, Now You Know fact boxes, a glossary and resources for further reading. | Summary: "This book looks at ways Cuba and the United States are alike and ways they differ. Readers will learn about Cuba's schools, holidays, music, and food."--Provided by publisher.

Identifiers: ISBN 9781634403283 (library hardcover) | ISBN 9781634403702 (paperback) | ISBN 9781634403337 (ebook)

Subjects: LCSH: Cuba--Social life and customs--Juvenile literature. | Cuba--Description and travel--Juvenile literature. | United States--Social life and customs--Juvenile literature. | United States--Description and travel--Juvenile literature. | CYAC: Cuba--Social life and customs. | Cuba--Description and travel. | United States--Social life and customs. | United States--Description and travel.

Classification: LCC F1758.5 .C56 2019 (print) | LCC F1758.5 (ebook) | DDC 972.91 [E]--dc23

LCCN: 2017963406

Copyright © 2019 Red Chair Press LLC
RED CHAIR PRESS, the RED CHAIR and associated logos are registered trademarks of Red Chair Press LLC.

All rights reserved. No part of this book may be reproduced, stored in an information or retrieval system, or transmitted in any form by any means, electronic, mechanical including photocopying, recording, or otherwise without the prior written permission from the Publisher. For permissions, contact info@redchairpress.com

Photo credits: iStock except for the following; p. 17: Shutterstock; p. 18: Dreamstime

Printed in the United States of America

0918 1P CGS19

Table of Contents

All About Cuba	4
The Land	14
The People	16
Cuba's Animals	18
Celebrations	20
Words to Keep	22
Learn More at the Library	23
Index	24

All About Cuba

Cuba [COO-bah] is the largest **island** in the Caribbean (kuh-RIB-ee-uhn) Sea. Cuba is close to the tip of Florida. That means that Cuba and the United States are neighbors.

Good to Know

Cuba is long, but not very wide. You could drive across it in one hour!

Atlanta

Jacksonville

Orlando

Miami

Gulf of Mexico

North Atlantic Ocean

THE BAHAMAS

HAVANA

CUBA

HAITI

JAMAICA

Carribbean Sea

5

Cuba's flag has blue and white stripes. It has a red triangle with a star inside.

Good to Know

The flag of the United States is also red, white, and blue. How are the two flags different?

7

The **capital** of Cuba is Havana. Havana is Cuba's largest city. About 2 million people live here.

Good to Know

Some Cubans drive U.S. cars that are from the 1950s. Wow!

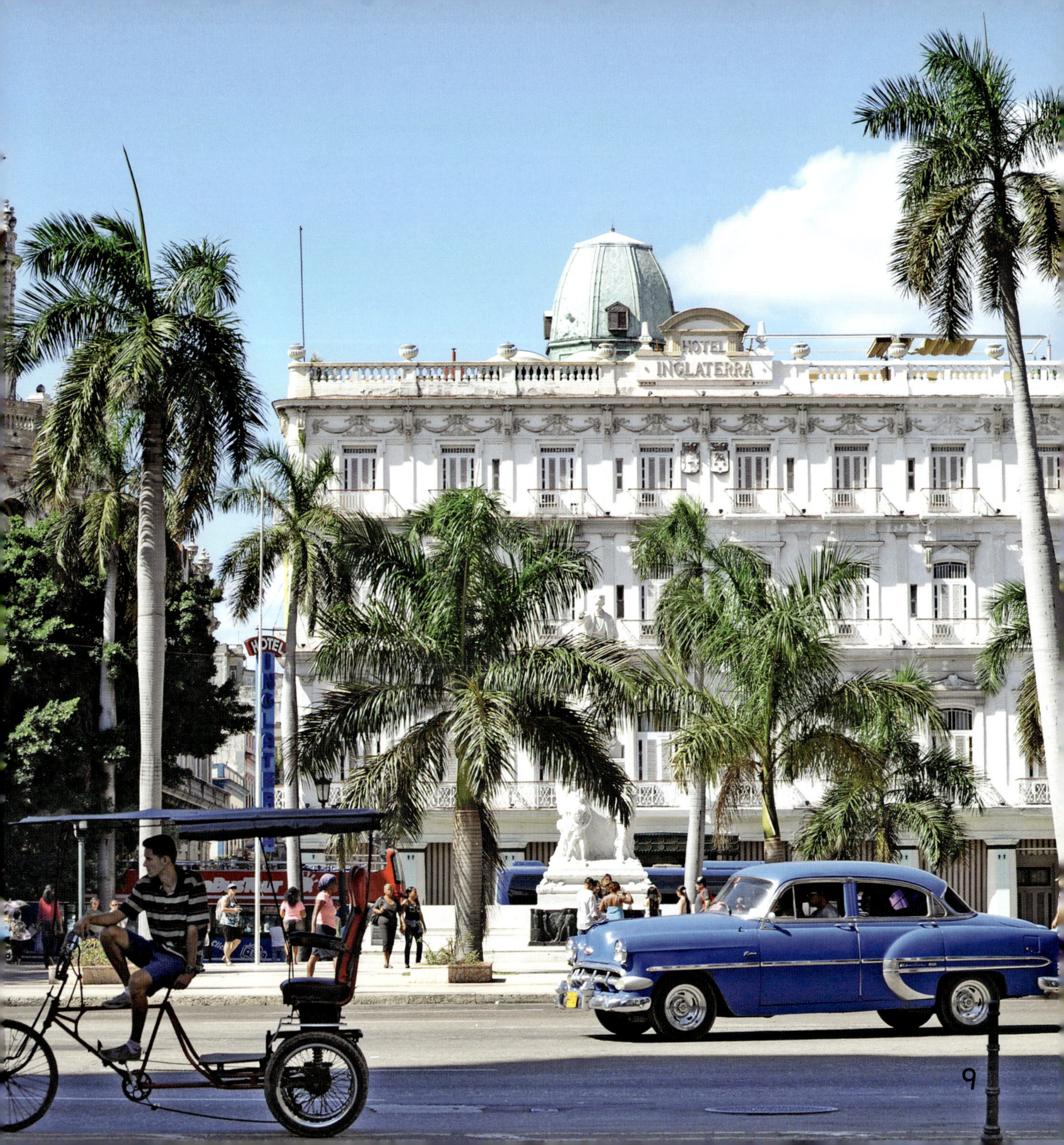
HOTEL
INGLATERRA
HOTEL
INGLATERRA

The man shown on this bill is a Cuban hero. Cuban coins and bills are called *Cuban Pesos.* [PAY-sohz]

The most popular sport in Cuba is baseball. Many baseball players in the U.S. come from Cuba.

Good to Know

Can you name a hero who is shown on American money?

11

The **national** bird of Cuba is the Cuban *trogon*, which is red, white, and blue—just like Cuba's flag!

The national tree is the tall royal palm. This tree can grow to 100 feet (30 meters) high. In heavy winds, it drops its leaves to stay tall.

The trogon, also called the *tocororo*, is found only in Cuba.

The Land

Cuba is a **tropical** island. The temperature stays warm all year. It snowed only once in Cuba—way back in 1857!

Good to Know

Sugar from sugar cane is Cuba's most important crop.

15

The People

Cubans come from a mix of cultures: Native Indian, Spanish, African—even Chinese!

Cuban music, called *son*, is a mix of African drums, Spanish guitars, and lively beats. In the U.S., we call this music *salsa*.

Good to Know

The words *canoe* and *barbecue* come from the Taíno Indians. These native people lived on Cuba hundreds of years ago.

Cuba's Animals

The bee hummingbird is the world's smallest bird. To many Cubans, this bird is a sign of love.

The Mount Iberia frog is so small it can sit on your fingernail with room to spare!

The Cuban iguana is a kind of lizard. It looks like it belongs in a scary movie!

Cuba's flamingos are bright pink. They have comb-like filters in their bills. The filters help the birds sort food from water.

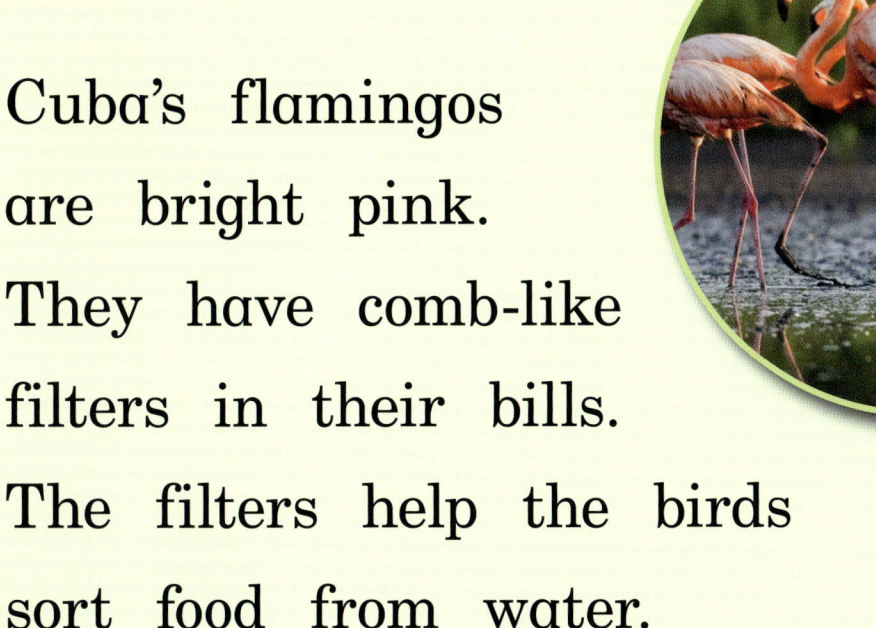

Cuban tree snails have colorful shells. Children collect these shells, just as U.S. children collect shells at the beach.

Celebrations

June 1 is <u>Children's Day</u>. This is a day to honor children. Children celebrate at school and in the streets. They dance folk dances.

Good to Know

Children wear white, red, and blue clothes to school each day.

21

Words to Keep

capital: city where a nation's government is based

carnival: a public celebration

Christopher Columbus: first European believed to sail to North America in 1492

island: land that has water all around it

national: belonging to a nation

tropical: a part of Earth that is hot, humid, and damp

Learn More at the Library

Books (Check out these books to learn more.)

Conley, Kate. *Cuba*. The Child's World, 2016.

Doak, Robin S. *Cuba* (First Reports). Compass Point Books, 2004.

Moon, Walter K. *Let's Explore Cuba* (Bumba Books). Lerner, 2017.

Web Sites (Ask an adult to show you this web site.)

National Geographic for Kids
https://www.natgeokids.com/uk/discover/geography/countries/cuba-facts/

Index

baseball	10–11
bee hummingbird	20–21
Children's Day	20–21
Cuban trogon	12–13
flag	6–7
Havana	8–9
royal palm	12–13
sugarcane	14

About the Author

Jeri Cipriano has written and edited many books for young readers. She likes making new friends from different places. Jeri lives and writes in New York state.